Princess and Fairy

Anna Pignataro

Princess and Fairy were friends forever,
And they did everything together:

Giggles and fun at Briar Wood School,
Twice-creams by the Dragonfly Pool,

Midnight treats and secret wishes,
Toadstool dancing and fairy swishes,

Hide'n'seek at Ladybird Bend,
Best of friends to the fairy end!

One morning while baking cupcakes galore,
A letter flew up from under the door.
They spotted the Queen's unmistakable seal,
And Princess and Fairy both let out a squeal!

"Tonight," they cried, "pretty things indeed!
Let's make a list of all that we need."
Promptly they primped for their royal occasion,
Then wrote their list and ran to the station.

Princess and Fairy skip down the lane,
And hop on the bumbling Beetlebug Train.
Three Wishes Market has marvellous things –
Smudges of fairy dust, feathery wings!

Can you

find?

"Here is a map of all you can see,"
Says Whiskers the Wizard while giggling with glee.
Where shall they start when there's so much to do?
"Best keep moving," says Mr Toowoo.

Gold Penny Lane is chock-a-block –
Not a chair to spare at the twice-cream shop,
Too frantic by far for a Fairy Flow Spa,
(Where all good fairies go to polish their stars!)

Trillions of dresses in all the right hues,
Hats and tiaras and sparkly shoes.
"Goodness," says Princess, "there's so much to find,
The list is so long and we've only found five!"

For breath-shaking rides and licorice lace,
Fairyland Fairground is just the right place!
Princess and Fairy float up and then down
On the Topsy Turvy Fairy-Go-Round.

Can you

Their fur is all tumbled, their tummies are tizzy,
They can't feel so dizzy, they're awfully busy!
"I'll take you to town, just hop on my saddle."
Thank goodness for Nixie – don't diddle or daddle!

Witch Whistle flies high above the town,
While Churchyard Beetle scuttles around.
The Twinkleclock chimes – oh dear, the time!
Eight pretty things they still have to find!

Can you

A naughty old wind shakes Fairy's wand free,
And whirls it away past the Library Tree.
They're sure to find something enchanting up there,
But Princess and Fairy have no time to spare!

From Slippery Hill Princess and Fairy can see
Ruby Rabbit, her carrots and old Potter Bee.
Piggeldy Moss is world-famous for mud,
And Princess and Fairy fall in with a thud!

"My dress," cries Princess, "my socks and my shoes!"
"My goodness," sobs Fairy, "I'm all messy too."
"No time for fuss," warns Ravencroft May,
"You must run along, you haven't all day!"

It's almost dark, the stars skip about,
The party has started without a doubt.
They creep down the path where the Story House grows,
Perhaps Miss Cricket will know where to go?

Can you

What an amazing sight at Lulu's Lair –
Such wonderful treasures piled everywhere!
They search high and low and quick as a wink,
Find the prettiest thing – something that's PINK!

"Your majesty," says Fairy, "we must declare
These pretty things we found to share.
We really hope you can excuse,
Our freckled frocks and grubby shoes..."

"Oh my, you are two speckled messes,
But never mind your dirty dresses.
Your smiles," says the Fairy Queen,
"Are the prettiest things I've ever seen!"

Because they've tried their very best,
The Fairy Queen is most impressed.
She gives them a glowing wish to share,
Inside a bubble of angel air.

Princess and Fairy, mud and all,
Together hold their wishing ball.
With one big breath and one sweet thought,
They blow their wish as they've been taught . . .

. . . Beneath the glimmer of shimmery cloud,
They find their friends all smiling proud.

They sparkle like the brightest stars,
Today has been the best by far.

The End